DEDICATION

To the apples of my eye, Jackson Karter, Kairo Shakur and Kaz Hendrix, you all are the reason why I work so hard.

To my best friend and the vessel of life for our children, Khadeen, you are the epitome of excellence, the microcosm of my ultimate happiness and I vow to do everything in my power to provide and protect us all.

I love you guys.

THE ELLISES & THE TIME MACHINE:
WHY DO WE HAVE TO SAY
«BLACK LIVES MATTER?»

Written by: Devale Ellis | Illustrated by: HH-Pax

It was the perfect Saturday afternoon in Brooklyn at the Ellis home. Nine-year-old Jackson and his father, Devale, were watching the basketball game in the living room when Jackson curiously asked, "Yo Pops! Why do we have to say 'Black Lives Matter?' Doesn't everyone know that?"

"You would think so," said Devale. "But isn't it racist to only say 'Black Lives Matter'?" asked Jackson.

Devale turned off the TV and turned to Jackson. "'Black Lives Matter' doesn't mean that ONLY Black Lives Matter!"

Khadeen walked into the living room with 3-year-old Kaz on her hip and 4-year-old Kairo on her tail. "Why are you screaming as if there were a fire, Devale?" asked Khadeen.

Because I'm dealing with something more dangerous than a fire," said Devale. "Alright, everybody head to Jackson's room. It's time for a history lesson!"

"History is boring!" said Jackson. "I'm too young for history lessons" said Kairo, shaking his head. "Well," said Khadeen, "how do you expect to know where you're going if you don't know how you got here?"

"That's right! And history is never boring when you're learning the truth" said Dev-ale, excitingly.

Devale ran to Jackson's room in excitement.

"I can't believe we're missing the game for a history lesson," Jackson said. "You and your big mouth, Jackson!" said Kairo.

Devale was super excited because he knew that the boys had no clue what was behind the closet doors!

As Devale opened the closet doors, a huge, bright light followed by a gust of wind finally got everyone's attention!

Jackson jumped up, "What the..."
Khadeen cut him off before he could even think of finishing his sentence, "Watch your mouth, boy!"
Kairo jumped in, "Daddy is that a..."
"A TIME MACHINE!" said Devale.

Wow, the inside of the closet that holds Jackson's clothes and sneakers now looks like a spaceship! Khadeen buckled Kaz in and made her way to the cockpit.

"This time machine is only accessible with parental guidance. Buckle up, it's time for an adventure!" said Khadeen.

Khadeen typed in the year "1619" as Devale raised his hand high and yelled "COUNTDOWN! We all say 'truth' on 1!" The family counted down together, "3...2...1... TRUUUTTTHHHH" as Khadeen smashed the big red button!

With warp speed, the family zoomed to a different
dimension where 1619 was the present day.

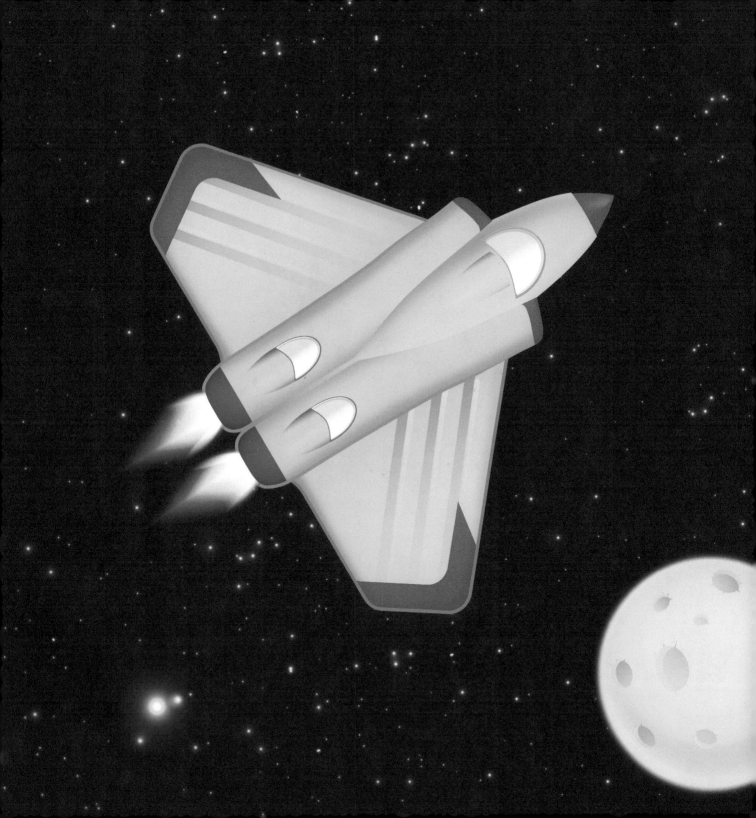

Slavery: In August of 1619 a ship settled on the shores of Fort Monroe in Hampton, Virginia. An English nobleman by the name of Robert Rich unloaded approximately 20 African captives off the White Lion ship.

This sparked a huge turning point in chattel slavery in America. Chattel slavery was legal under the law and allowed for enslaved Africans to be bought and sold as property for free labor.

Civil War: From 1861 to 1865, the northern states, known as The Union, and the southern states, known as The Confederates, fought over slavery and state rights. The seven Confederate states (South Carolina, Mississippi, Florida, Alabama, Georgia, Louisiana and Texas) wanted to continue to own slaves and expand slavery into the West following the election of President Abraham Lincoln. The Confederacy declared war with the hopes of starting their own country, but ultimately lost to The Union. Lincoln signed the Emancipation Proclamation in 1863, which symbolized the freedom of enslaved Africans. Congress formally passed the 13th Amendment to abolish slavery two and a half years later in 1865. The Union Army entered Texas on June 19, 1865 to mark the end of the civil war and enforce the abolishment of slavery. Today, this day is known as Juneteenth.

The Vagrancy Act: Although formerly enslaved Africans were now "free," a law was put in place in Virginia, then followed throughout the Confederate states, that forced any person who appeared to be unemployed or homeless to work in plantations. This law directly targeted newly freed Blacks looking to rebuild their lives after the war in 1866. The Vagrancy Act remained a law until 1904.

Black Codes: Although the Confederate South lost the Civil War, its leaders waged a political wa[r] on the freedom of Black people. In late 1865 into 1866, southern states like Mississippi and Sout[h] Carolina began enforcing laws which made it mandatory for Blacks to work under labor contract[s] and carry written documentation. Newly freed southern Blacks were at risk of being arrested an[d] getting into forced labor again. They were not allowed to vote, carry weapons for protection, gathe[r] in groups for worship, or learn how to read or write. Although northern and western states did n[ot] en[fo]rce the exact laws, many discouraged free Blacks from residing there.

Jim Crow. During the Reconstruction Era, the former Confederate states created laws that demanded separate public spaces based on race. These spaces included restrooms, restaurants, schools, libraries and public transportation. In 1896 the U.S. Supreme Court used the Plessy vs. Ferguson case to uphold the "Separate but Equal" doctrine after the Reconstruction Era. The facilities for Blacks were rarely equal as the majority were either underfunded, inhumane or nonexistent. In fact, many public places in the south refused to create separate accommodations for Blacks, or refused them access altogether. Racial segregation by Jim Crow laws were considered constitutional until they were overruled by the Civil Rights Act of 1964 and the Voting Rights Act of 1965.

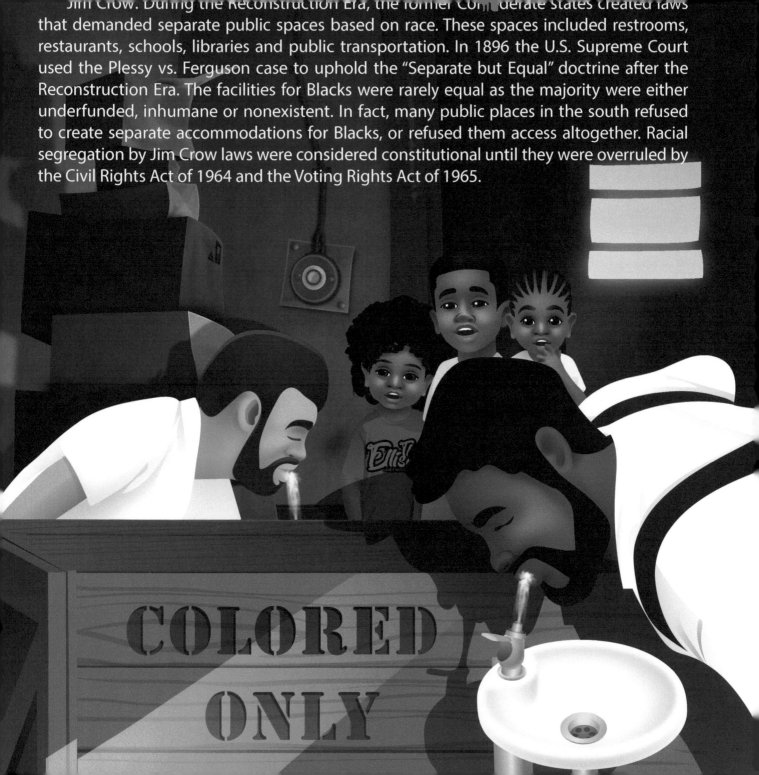

Klu Klux Klan: In the mid-1860s, the KKK formed to prevent Black people from gaining political power and sought to suppress their rights. The group upheld white supremacy by using voter intimidation and targeting violence towards Blacks, now known as African Americans. This secret organization was composed of southern white men that often wore white robes, face masks, and burned crosses to evoke intimidation.

Convict Leasing: Many southern leaders in government and in business wanted to find a new way to make money after chattel slavery ended in 1865. As slavery was now illegal, several states used the Vagrancy Act and other Black Codes to imprison free Black people, forcing them to work for free as prisoners in the southern states. Convict leasing existed in America under different names until it was abolished on December 12, 1941.

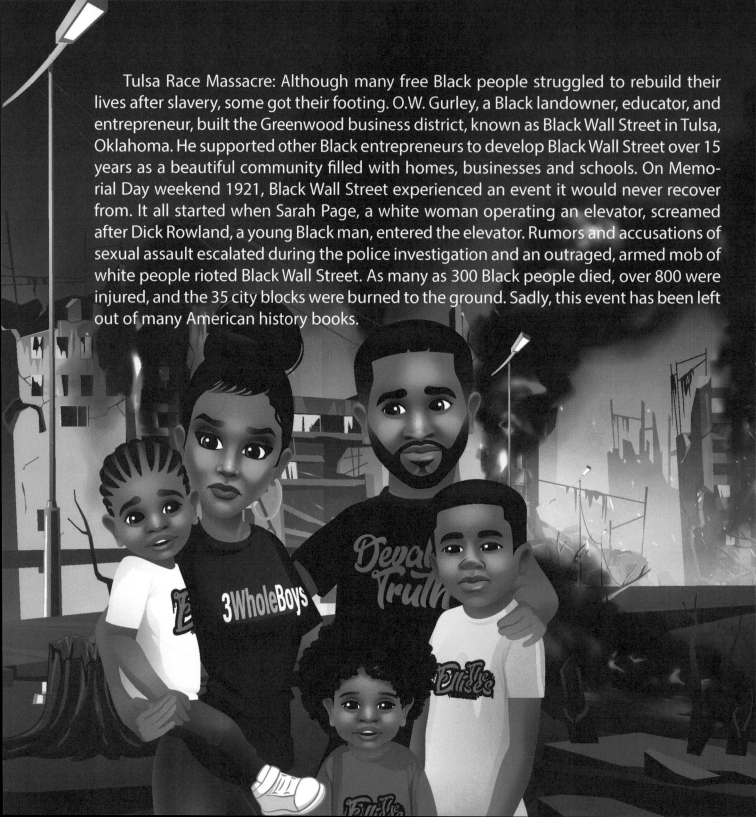

Tulsa Race Massacre: Although many free Black people struggled to rebuild their lives after slavery, some got their footing. O.W. Gurley, a Black landowner, educator, and entrepreneur, built the Greenwood business district, known as Black Wall Street in Tulsa, Oklahoma. He supported other Black entrepreneurs to develop Black Wall Street over 15 years as a beautiful community filled with homes, businesses and schools. On Memorial Day weekend 1921, Black Wall Street experienced an event it would never recover from. It all started when Sarah Page, a white woman operating an elevator, screamed after Dick Rowland, a young Black man, entered the elevator. Rumors and accusations of sexual assault escalated during the police investigation and an outraged, armed mob of white people rioted Black Wall Street. As many as 300 Black people died, over 800 were injured, and the 35 city blocks were burned to the ground. Sadly, this event has been left out of many American history books.

Red Lining: In 1934 during the Great Depression, The National Housing Act was enacted to address housing instability. The Federal Housing Administration was established to launch a mortgage insurance program, which consequently led to further segregation and gaps in fair opportunities between white and Black communities. The new housing market provided more housing and neighborhood improvements for white middle-class and lower-middle-class families, while pushing Black families into urban housing projects. Additionally, housing credit for mortgages in Black neighborhoods was often denied. Special benefits were extended to real estate developers who were building neighborhoods for white Americans with the understanding that no homes could be sold to Black people. This promoted segregation and contributed to the wealth gap seen today.

Police Brutality: In 1954 during the Civil Rights Movement, Black Americans began experiencing extreme physical violence at the hands of the local police. These attacks were photographed and caught on camera while protesters demonstrated nonviolent resistance and civil disobedience. Local governments often militarized their police forces against nonviolent Black protesters, using water hoses, dogs, batons and excessive force that resulted in physical assaults, numerous arrests and deaths.

The Black Panther Party: After decades of using civil disobedience and nonviolent protests to combat racial injustices and police brutality, The Black Panther Party for Self-Defense was created by college students, Bobby Seale and Huey Newton, in 1966. The core purpose of this group was to empower and protect Black neighborhoods against police brutality. In response to the Black Panther Party, the U.S. FBI director J. Edgar Hoover led and developed a program called COINTELPRO to discredit and criminalize the party. COINTELPRO was a counter-intelligence program responsible for causing major internal conflicts within the Party and the assassination of many influential Party leaders, like Fred Hampton and Mark Clark.

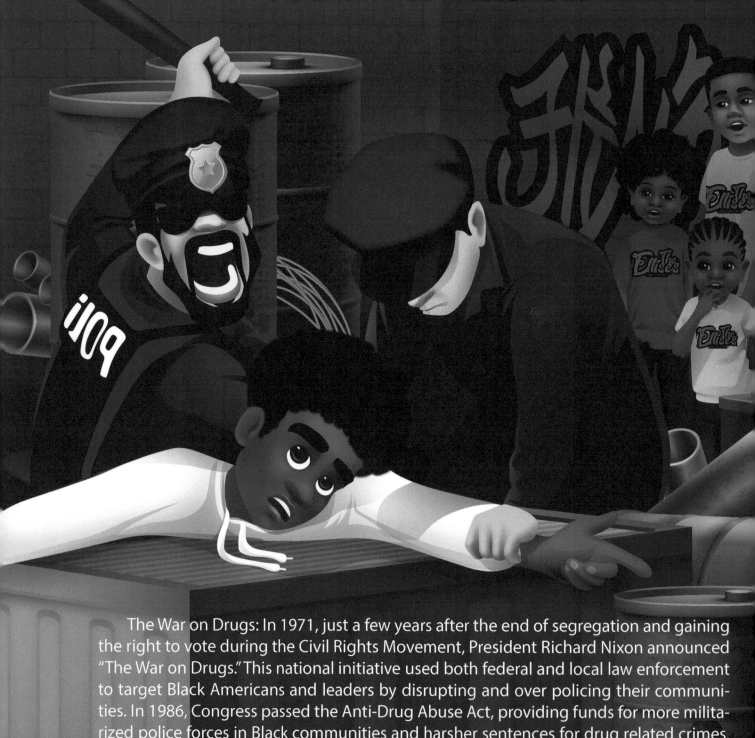

The War on Drugs: In 1971, just a few years after the end of segregation and gaining the right to vote during the Civil Rights Movement, President Richard Nixon announced "The War on Drugs." This national initiative used both federal and local law enforcement to target Black Americans and leaders by disrupting and over policing their communities. In 1986, Congress passed the Anti-Drug Abuse Act, providing funds for more militarized police forces in Black communities and harsher sentences for drug related crimes. This created soaring arrest rates for Black people.

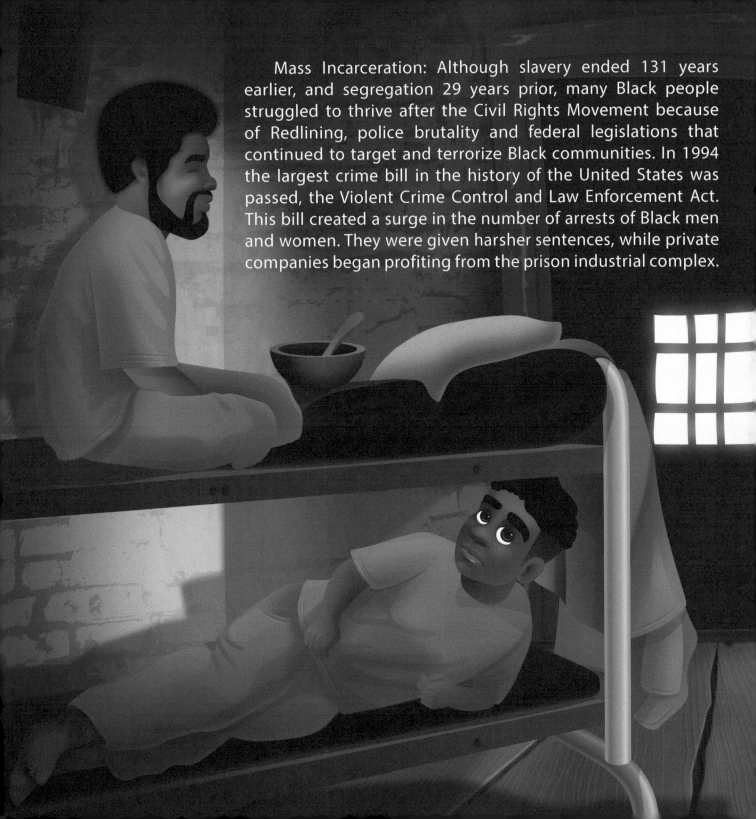

Mass Incarceration: Although slavery ended 131 years earlier, and segregation 29 years prior, many Black people struggled to thrive after the Civil Rights Movement because of Redlining, police brutality and federal legislations that continued to target and terrorize Black communities. In 1994 the largest crime bill in the history of the United States was passed, the Violent Crime Control and Law Enforcement Act. This bill created a surge in the number of arrests of Black men and women. They were given harsher sentences, while private companies began profiting from the prison industrial complex.

Black Lives Matter: In July 2013, the Black Lives Matter movement was created by Alicia Garza, Opal Tometi and Patrisse Cullors after the state of Florida failed to convict the murderer of an unarmed 17-year-old Black boy, Trayvon Martin, using the state's "Stand Your Ground" law. The Black Lives Matter movement mobilizes where youth meet most - on social media - and is a declaration to revolt against police brutality and a corrupt criminal justice system that profiles, targets, profits off of, and oftentimes kills Black Americans without consequence.

"Hey babe," said Khadeen, "I think it's time to get back." "Okay Ellises, time to go back," said Devale. The family put on their glasses and Devale hit the red button. A huge white flash appeared and the Ellises were instantly home.

Now back in Jackson's room after a journey that covered over 400 years, Devale said, "So you see, we say 'Black Lives Matter' to remind America that they forgot about us when they said 'with Liberty and Justice for ALL!'"

"So all we are asking for is equality, right Pops?" asked Jackson.

"Yeah bro. It's crazy that we still have to ask for it!" said Devale.

Jackson runs to open his closet. "Hey! Where ya going?" asked Khadeen. "The history lesson is over. You don't want to finish watching the game with your dad?"

"Are you kidding me? We need change and I can't change anything while watching a game! We need action!" exclaimed Jackson.

"Yeah!" said Kairo.

"Yeah!" said Kaz, speaking for the first time.

Jackson pushed his mom and dad out of the room and closed the door. "Do you think I shared too much?" Devale asked Khadeen. "Not at all! If they're anything like you, they'll work together to change the world for the better" said Khadeen, as she gave Devale a warm hug.

"We got work to do, gentlemen!" said Jackson.
"YEEEAAAHHHH!!!" screamed Kairo and Kaz in unison.

ABOUT THE AUTHOR:

Devale Ellis is a former NFL player turned actor, currently a series regular in the role of Zac on the #1 cable television drama series, *Tyler Perry's Sistas*. He appeared as a series regular in the Netflix series, *It's Bruno*, and in the recurring role of Ken on *Will Packer's BIGGER*.

Devale has appeared in guest starring roles on popular hit TV dramas such as *NCIS: Los Angeles, Power, The Blacklist, The Mysteries Of Laura, Gotham* and *The Breaks*, and played his first supporting role as Tommy in the award-winning feature film, *Full Circle*.

In addition to being a full-time actor, the Brooklynite is the co-host of *Dead Ass with Khadeen & Devale*, a Webby award-winning podcast that he created with his wife to discuss love, marriage, parenting and everything in between from a millennial perspective. The podcast launched in the spring of 2019 and hit #5 on the Apple charts its first day and has remained top 10 since, securing 4 sold out live shows and over 10 million downloads, with notable guests including Presidential Elect, Joe Biden. His viral social show, *The Ellises*, has garnered over 300 million views across YouTube and Facebook.

Prior to his booming career as an actor and public personality, Devale and his brother Brian founded Elite Prototype Athletics, a New York-based organization created to give back to the city that raised them, designed to educate and train student athletes to encompass the tools needed to succeed in life on and off the field. The organization has grown to mentor over 500 student athletes from ages 8-25, with its first class of students entering the NFL draft in 2012, with several signing NFL contracts.

Devale is a graduate of Hofstra University and lives a bi-coastal life, residing in both California and New York with his wife, Khadeen, and their three children, Jackson, Kairo and Kaz.

VISIT

www.mcbridestories.com

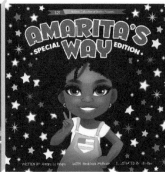

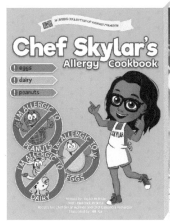

CPSIA information can be obtained
at www.ICGtesting.com
Printed in the USA
BVHW020220181220
595889BV00006B/7